Since giving up professional cookery, Robbie Brown has been working on his true ambition and finding his niche as a writer. Born in Glasgow, he has lived in Dundee, the South of France (near where D.H. Lawrence died) and now resides in the 'Colony of Artists' in Edinburgh's Abbeyhill area.

erbr88sj

To Mum & Gregor

Robbie Brown

SURREAL JOURNEY

AUSTIN MACAULEY PUBLISHERS™

LONDON • CAMBRIDGE • NEW YORK • SHARJAH

A CIP catalogue record for this title is available from the British Library.

ISBN 9781398447707 (Paperback)
ISBN 9781398447714 (ePub e-book)

www.austinmacauley.com

First Published 2023
Austin Macauley Publishers Ltd®
1 Canada Square
Canary Wharf
London
E14 5AA

Thanks to the publishers at Austin Macauley for having faith in something that could have lain in a box for all time. Much of this book was inspired by the music of Sune Rose Wagner.

1

Many men are disillusioned souls. Such men are not necessarily heroes, even if they are capable of extraordinary heroism and bravery within them. Indeed, the man whose scribblings are contained here, was no kind of hero. Simply, a misguided man, with aspirations of genius and innovation, that he could never match up to, keeping him trapped among ghouls, murderers and demons, or so he would claim. Perhaps the reality would merely see him suffering from an imaginary psychosis that only affects disillusioned revellers. Whatever anyone, himself included, thought he may be, at times he certainly felt like the loneliest of men.

This loneliness had formed from a sense of detachment, growing into isolation over time. He became unable to connect with anyone and would fixate on things, finding it impossible to relax or feel free, unless he was by himself, obsessing over something. In spite of his own good judgement, he had taken to writing personal, private (and ultimately hopeless) love letters.

The subject of many of these letters was a Spanish girl named Lara. Lara was a fine girl with typically dark, enchanting eyes usually imagined on princesses. She had a fantastic energy and aura, and was happy to get on with everyone she could. This was where the fascination with Lara was born, in that she was the smiling antithesis to his morbid hopelessness and increasing seclusion. Not that he was terrifically well acquainted with her, for all he knew she would return to her bed at night and lament her own life, dreaming of home, the way he was doing now. All travellers must feel at some moments, however far or near, the tinges of homesickness always kick in now and again.

All things, surely, can be traced back to one principal catalyst. When this man decided to take a journey across the sea, absconding in a fit of desperation to prove that romance and love could still blossom in today's world, he elected to take a journey into himself, to explore the very darkest parts of his being. And some of the very darkest parts of the world. Not that he knew this yet. This world of pubs and clubs had created a weariness to mar his disillusion. The status quo and repetitiveness of his life, the loss of all sense of fun and joy finally got to him after spending yet another weekend out in this drug-fuelled, anger-drenched society of recklessness.

His conscience, once a guiding light within him, told him it was time to discover something else. Something that didn't seek to fall in line with the drudgery, the uniformity. It was this uniformity and the overemphasis on glossiness that caused his weary sighs in those particular hours, the absolute similarity of it all. Hundreds of people who looked the same, doing the same, acting the same. How uninspired, uninventive, closed-off would they have to become before the government simply decided to lobotomise them all? The majority of people were halfway there anyway.

If life was some pursuit of a greater, truer, higher love, then somewhere along the line, people had given up the effort and simply decided to compromise, settle for everything they were spoon fed. We will like what we are told to and look no further into ourselves to question it. We will delight in every hyperbole and accept every lie. The truth and true love is far too terrifying for us, let us revel in our tiny locked minds.

He was overwhelmed with sarcastic bitterness and scoffed at this idea, this image of today's youth.

Here, amongst these doomed souls, people who seem as if they were put together on an assembly line rather than being born, programmed to conform to every stereotype and engage in every stupidity.

'This is fun because we are told this is how to have fun.' Not an original idea or thought amongst them. He stood alone, in a silent protest that was more against himself than anything. For too long, he had joined in with this obedient idiocy, no more.

The time had come for him to get apart from these people, his supposed peers. He grew angry and felt true disgust at their fixations on looks, status, style, mascara, falsehoods and abortions of all kinds. They were living it, their own brain-dead abortion.

As the song faded down and his distressed mind cooled for a moment, a rare gap in the DJ set saw a tender electro-love ballad followed by a rousing, raw pop punk anthem that sent him straight to the seventies.

Reflecting on his oh-so-marvellous misery, a kindred spirit passed by, bouncing past him as she created her own enjoyment instead of remarking so bitterly on everyone else's preconceived notions of fun.

He was drawn to flamboyant, expressive characters on nights out and they seemed drawn to him, this particular one he would never know, yet her face and her spirit, captured for merely a split second in the flashing darkness, would stay with him for a long time.

She was living proof that for him, at least, happiness was an elusive animal he had given up laying traps for. He would bask in this misery as he plotted his eventual escape. The girl looked like an eighties bubble-gum pop singer and had he not been so uptight and angry that night, ashamed of his own sobriety, he may well have discovered that she was both an avid football fanatic (and talented at the game herself) an aspiring musician and highly – if confused – sexually charged. Furthermore, she held similar ideas on the state of today's youth and the self-important hipsters that populated, even dictated it. Every night she grooved apart from them, endlessly daydreaming.

The night ended and the next morning he awoke, long before everyone else, the friends and would-be lovers he now felt no connection with, no empathy for and no desire to ever be around. It wasn't their fault, they were happy in their dumb bliss, it was he who treaded in the waters of morbidity.

Half-heartedly, he made his way to a nearby cafe bar in an alley and half-heartedly watched a football match. The game itself lacking in real passion and intensity, but this was seen in the fans, heard and witnessed in their dedication to the cause and love of their respective teams. It made him appreciate the game all the more, even if he didn't enjoy it as much as he used to, yet another thing to become wilfully disenchanted with. He left as soon as the final whistle blew, as did the entire stadium.

And so his mind was made up to travel to the United States, for a length of time yet to be decided. Shortly before he departed, he and a friend took in a gig.

The would-be traveller found himself in awe and slightly in love with the group's keyboardist, a girl who exuded effortless cool, setting the tone of the crowd. He knew he should be enjoying himself and the music, looking forward to his trip but he could only fixate on the girl. Another girl, apart from all the rest, a celestial aura surrounding them, a burning desire and exuberance in them, hidden by a mask of cool.

Fixations on people or things we don't really know or understand are hard to relinquish, for the self-created mystery upon them can run and run. We can create images and scenarios for people we don't know ourselves and place them on a pedestal, simply from our own imaginations and expectations, how we perceive and imagine them to be. How we wish them to be, making idols and heroes from often undeserving beings, while ignoring the true greatness of others. Projections of the mind, that allow us to forget our own reality, place our fears, hopes and questions onto someone else. Live in their perception of reality that you, yourself, imagine.

If only he could know and understand this girl, whom he later found out to be from Brazil and called Ana, these discoveries fuelling the exotic mystique around her keyboard. They could change the world together, or so he imagined.

Music was his last, untainted source of hope. A pure joy. All kinds of music could touch your heart, strike that inexplicable chord, but so few possessed the power to pierce your soul. Only such a tiny, yet all-consuming, all-powerful voice could do so. A voice not unlike that of Billie Holiday's.

A voice that had been with him for much of his life, both his mother and father spent a lot of time playing Billie's records around the house.

A memory struck him, him and his mother in a restaurant for Mother's Day, over a year after the passing of his father. Midway through a conversation, the unmistakable velvet tones of Lady Day filled the restaurant, rising above the hum of conversations and rushing around, demanding and captivating attention. It should have been his mother who found herself nearly in tears but instead it was he, dumbstruck by the emotion resonating from essentially background music. There was an unnatural power in her voice and he knew he was not the first to be reduced to tears by it.

His mind-set the night before he took his trip across the Atlantic waved between a painful fear, a disturbing sense of hopelessness and the simple blues, all unbefitting a man who was about to make a journey into self-discovery. Perhaps he was fearful of what he might find there, that he would become further disillusioned, or that he was scared of what he might find within himself.

Unable to sleep, he caught most of the film, 'Lost in Translation', on late night TV, seeing it for the first time. Suitably cheered by the movie, it could be said that on that lonely night, the actress Scarlett Johansson had cured his blues. For the meantime at least.

Finding further comforting solitude in his record collection, he felt compelled to write a tribute; highlighting the wondrous art of music, a tribute he would add to, change and would not finally complete, until his return from America. For as yet, there was still one band out there for him to hear, a duo that would touch his soul in a way he could only dream of right now.

As he took his final moments wake, all the music he had ever heard in the world would have struggled to impact upon either his heart or his mind in any positive way. He feared for every male and female of every generation and minority. Something in the breeze told him the world was facing change of an explosive and incomprehensible nature. His lasting thought before sleep, before the journey, was that society would be the downfall of itself.

2

The traveller landed in what he hoped was America around ten o'clock in the evening local time. Sipping on coffee, he was still unable to shake from his mind the utter sorrow that so plagued it. The other side of the world he may be but it was still a world that was ending. This was supposed to be an adventure, yet he could only feel a sense of delaying the inevitable conclusion, that time was already running out on this romantic quest of self.

He was tempted in his frenzy of mind to turn back, go home now before he confronted the abyss, but he soon relaxed. His worries subsided (albeit briefly) and he felt at peace with things, it was almost like a spiritual intervention, for the sake of the quest. This would happen again.

Embracing American spirit by renting a Cadillac, our romantic explorer took to the backroads, still hurting deep within. As he drove, humanity's sorrowful shame appeared in the form of a group of homeless people, huddled round a large, burning metal can, fighting over scraps of food and dregs of wine, perhaps any remaining, fading scraps of dignity and pride too.

He could not help but drive slowly past and look, thinking about that kind of life, true loneliness and misery, the never-ending road, the way of the hobo.

After this he found himself with a huge stretch of open road to drive into and beyond. Just before embarking, he stopped by the side of the road and lit a cigarette. He had quit years ago but liked to keep a pack on him for so-called emergencies. Sometimes, a cigarette would help him think, this one doing just that, as he paced around his vehicle.

His mind was racing again, he was close to shaking with fear, with panic, with utter sadness dulling his insides. How could he possibly be on this foolish expedition to find himself or find romance, whatever he was vaguely looking for, when the world was in such decline and its peoples in such decay, both mentally and physically?

His continued wallowing had made his entire being, his heart, his legs, his mind, so very heavy and he concluded that driving across barren landscapes was not the right thing to do right now. Time to find the first motel of the trip.

It took him nearly forty-five minutes to see a glorious, neon, 'Vacancies' sign (glorious certainly when one is so tired and in such a weary state).

The shabbiness of the place could so easily be traded for character and the eeriness of the surroundings as quaint and peaceful, even in this pitch black. A good night's sleep could take care of the most restless minds and travellers. Picture any motel from any American road movie. Similar, aren't they?

Well this one looked exactly like you are picturing. Although extremely tired, sleep was hard to come by in this environment.

Around four am, he was jolted from his wandering thoughts by the sound of breaking glass, very loud Christmas music and hints of not screaming, but painful yelps.

Stepping out onto the front balcony, he saw a woman come running up the stairs and start banging on the door where the noises were coming from. She was shouting,

'Bobby Jean! What's going on? Are you okay?,' while from inside the room only a muffled, repetitive,

'Bitch!' could be heard over the misplaced merry, jingly tunes.

As he accepted no sleep would be got here tonight, he listened to the pleas of the banging fist and the heart-wrenching screams of the man a couple of doors along, obviously losing his mind as he screamed,

'She stole my heart!'

The long and barren road, stretched ever longer in his exhausted state, with only a passing, monstrous truck and scraps of roadkill for company. Barely able to keep his eyes open, he had no choice but to pull into what appeared to be a large, empty carpark. Unfortunately, with it being so dark, he failed to notice he was on the grounds of an abandoned funfair. The creak of old metal in the wind helped him drift off into sweet dreams on a deathly road.

When he woke from a most disturbing nightmare, he had no idea where he was. Although aware he had been dreaming, the vividness and stark lucidity of the horror, made it seem like a vision rather than subconscious, flashing images, as if he had been briefly gazing into a nuclear future.

He only felt safe, because he was sure he was dreaming now, such was the clearness of the voice of mankind's fiery demise. Settling back into what he was sure was reality, panic over, he remembered his reason for being there, his trip.

The time was nine thirty in the am and he set off again. Nearly another hour of driving passed, until he clocked a roadside bar that surely indicated a nearby town. Despite it still being relatively early in the morning, loud noises could be heard from within. Perhaps this was one of these places where partying goes on 24/7, out with the regular jurisdictions and etiquettes of closing times.

He stepped tepidly inside, not knowing what he would find. There were people, two men and a woman, dancing a bizarre, ritualistic dance by the jukebox in the corner of the room. A large, biker man passionately kissed an orange-haired lady on top of the pool table.

Our traveller sat at the bar, waiting for someone to emerge from the various facets of mayhem and serve him a drink. Moments later, a man with his face painted black and white stripes and a wicker holster, slung across his torso, lifted his sunglasses up, to reveal colourless eyes, not unlike those of an albino (perhaps he was) and smirked knowingly.

The increasingly petrified traveller found himself sipping on a thick, green liquid that began to warp different shades of reds and purples. Think of drinking a lava lamp. A ska-lite figure blared tunelessly on a small trumpet before bursting into insane giggles. There was a snake in a goldfish bowl behind the bar.

Onstage, a priest took the microphone from a searingly beautiful woman in red, who had been singing. Everyone ceased their individual, eccentric displays and fixed their eyes on the priest, who stood silent. The bar was, all of a sudden, a picture of calm. Soon they were all dancing to the same song, something unmistakably from the eighties, led by the father, his sleeves now rolled up and a pale, blue, furry top-hat donning his holy head. Smirking relentlessly, the man in the face paint grabbed a young blonde woman, who would not have looked out of place in a 1950s American high school, and stabbed her in the shoulder with an arrow.

The room began to spin and all its revellers took on horrifying, otherworldly, bestial apparitions. The priest fired a gun and all hell broke loose.

Again, he could not be quite sure whether he had actually seen, hallucinated or merely been dreaming these murderous creatures and their individual stories, for whatever was in his multi-coloured drink was sure to be ludicrously potent. Whatever the truth, these visions of anthropomorphic animals and holy leaders at war through the centuries, appearing to him like a twisted sketch show, sound tracked by the blaring of obscure musical instruments, would haunt him for the longest time.

Though he could never repeat his visions to anyone. Whether true or not, premonitions, liquor-fuelled reflections or just dreams, were too far into the realms of impossible horror and insanity. The sights and sounds of that bar were so horrendous, so full of evil that he had completely blacked out and found himself miles down the road, asleep in his rented automobile.

It had started to snow, not white and wonderful, but so grey and flaky, that it seemed like it could be the ashes of vanquished ghosts.

Was it even really snowing?

He queried to himself, struggling to remove himself from his state of disbelief and horror. Suddenly, it fully dawned on him, alone and effectively lost somewhere in America, that fairly soon it would be Christmas time. He thought about his mother, wondering if her only son would be at home this Christmas.

At first, he feared the car wouldn't start and he would be stranded in this snowy, lonely wasteland that could really be anywhere. When the car eventually got going, it became evident that the vehicle itself was in control, taking him to God knows where. Whatever twists and turns the car decided to take, they would not stop before nightfall.

3

Nightfall duly came and brought with it more snow. It soon became apparent to the traveller that continuing to drive was no longer an option, despite what the automobile wanted. They would have to stop somewhere and see it through, but where? He had seen absolutely nothing for miles except darkness and weather. And this weather was becoming a full-scale blizzard.

Until, a light in the distance! A beacon of hope calling him out! Towards the light he drove, surely for some much-needed rest. Weary and frightened, his heart sank as the turn-in nearest to the light was onto a pier and the light was that of a lighthouse. Hoping against hope, he flashed his lights as he realised fuel was perilously low.

He shivered, *hope was lost...or was it?*

A small yet growing light appeared to be coming toward him, unless this was another vision, more demons out to bring hell to earth. It was no vision, nor a demon. The light was a lantern, held by a hooded figure who rapped on the driver's side window, identifying himself as the lighthouse keeper. Not a devil, just one lonely, lighthouse keeper.

This particular lonely, lighthouse keeper, the weary road tripper was pleasantly surprised to find, hailed from Scotland.

Rough as the seas he watched over each night, he gave the impression of a man, who one day wanted the world (most likely in his youth, so perhaps not so unlike our traveller himself) but had been given only this small corner of it to guard and protect.

He brewed some tea and rolled a cigarette from extremely pungent tobacco. They swapped a few stories, the traveller relaying the path that had led him through a blizzard and to the lighthouse. The guardian of the ocean pointed his trusty lantern to the north-east direction of the pier.

'See that area of black lookin' trees over there? That is no ordinary forest.' His monotonous, gruff Highland tones were assuring and comforting, a reminder of his adopted homeland across the pond.

'This tobacco your nostrils are no doubt reeling from, the tea that is about to sting your throat, both grow over there. They call it the Unforgiven Forest, although it probably should be 'unforgiving' by all accounts. Only the bravest souls venture in there, the goings-on are said to be quite mysterious.'

He took short pauses between the last two words, possibly for effect, possibly from a brief mental relapse into some harrowing tales. Either way it couldn't be true.

An enchanted forest? Complete and utter madness. Then again, the preceding events of that hellish, karaoke jam proved, that out in this wilderness, almost anything could be believed.

And so, he decided, he must join the brave few and venture in. He thanked the lighthouse keeper for his hospitality, who responded with only a faint nod and turned back to the sea, sipping gingerly on his steaming mug of forest tea, barely noticing when his 'guest' had gone. Did he fear for him in some way?

The ground had turned frosty and hard, each step crunching the brittle grass as if tiny peoples lived beneath it. Far in the distance, stood an eerie old cottage. Taking in his surroundings carefully, he made certain he had not doubled back to the lighthouse or his mind playing more evil tricks on him. Satisfied the cottage was not an illusion, he crept towards it, carefully avoiding to tread on twigs on the ground for such a noise could echo crystal clear in this solemn wood.

Was that a light bouncing around through the window? A candle perhaps?

Could there be people living in there, here? His eyes were now adjusting to the darkness, like a child who had been screaming for the light to be left on at night, finally accepting it was time for sleepy-sleeps.

Gradually, he got close enough to surreptitiously peer in the window, where he witnessed a mermaid engaged in a sex act with a gun-toting figure in colourful makeup.

Finding himself a small alcove of a fallen tree to take refuge in, he tried not to believe he was part of a macabre fairy-tale.

It was now tremendously cold. The kind of cold where you would shiver violently, to accentuate how cold it actually was, as if someone was watching you in some far-off crystal ball. He knew no-one was watching him so ceased this act, yet remained shivering helplessly. It was agonisingly cold. And deathly dark.

After seeing the light of the house, his eyes again needed time to adjust. There was no possibility of him sleeping here, for he would surely die. No choice now, but to attempt, somehow, to make his way out of the forest.

He had ran so far, from where he had wandered in, that realistically, he was lost. The trees offered no pathway or direction, so he walked aimlessly until he noticed a glow, weaving itself in and out of the unhelpful trees.

What on earth was this to be?

The glowing slowed to a motionless still, except for the flickering of its own outline that is the nature of a glowing in the dark. Were there any proper lights here or merely hints and flickers of such? He had to remind himself that he was in the middle of a forest.

Peering at it from behind a tree, about ten feet away, he wondered if he should call out to it. Even if there was no actual being or living organism within it, it was feasible that it could still lead him out of here.

Could the glow see him?

It began to move again, towards him. His instincts and desperation to get out of this place told him to follow the glow, which still displayed no signs of actual life. After walking a little while more, the glow disappeared and he came across a deathly-looking woman sitting on a fallen tree, eating some sort of small animal which bizarrely enough turned out to be a fish.

Quite how she came to acquire a fish (for they must be a long way away from the ocean by now) he could not fathom. The ghostly woman ignored him or simply did not register his presence, his intrusion on her land. She simply sat, eating her raw fish. Nothing else could gain her attention, until a rabbit scurried past. Like a predatory feline, her eyes grew large and her whole body stood on end. In a flash she took an object –

a small spear of some kind – from the string belt that tied her floating white dress, to her pale, thin body and launched it at the rabbit, killing it instantly. After a second or so, looking at her kill, she went back to her fish. The snow began to fall again, the huntress ignoring this too.

It had not occurred to him that his own life may well be in danger. The woodland woman could just as easily murder him, should she ever take notice of his being there. Bravely, he sat within three feet of her as she ate, the strangest situation of being an unwelcome dinner guest he could possibly imagine.

He felt as if she may have glanced at him ever so slightly but was afraid of making eye contact with her. His mind wandered into the great beyond, the vault in his imagination unlocked. Among these forest dwellers, could it be said that they were human?

A mermaid woman – seemingly a sex-slave to a madman and a ghostly elfin lady with a talent for murder and bloodlust. He began to think of all human beings as empty vessels at the very beginning of their existence, drifting between worlds until their soul is complete and able to rest. The process and the journey could take any number of lifetimes, perhaps some would never be at peace.

Doomed to wander aimlessly, twitching restlessly in the night, only their nightmares and vague, hazy memories for company. We are never so alone and nothing seems so important to us as those all-consuming fears in the depths of the night.

There is something about that dark, lonely world that causes the mind to run riot. Realising now that his belongings in the rented Cadillac were most probably lost or stolen, the lighthouse keeper no doubt presuming him dead, eaten by the ghostly elfin murderess.

At least he had the good sense to retain his identification and monetary cards on his person, so that if he ever were to escape the forest, he could eat, sleep and make his way home.

So deep in his own thoughts, he had not noticed the elf lady get up from her seat on the tree and begin to walk into the clearing and up the frosty hill. Clearly his presence was either unseen, or she had no interest in him as prey, so he followed her in the hope she would somehow take him to a way out.

She took small, pacing steps, silent on the crisp, thin grass as if wary of being there, at some moments almost gliding through the fog that had taken over duties from the snowfall for the backshift. Such was the surreal nature of being alone in a forest inhabited by such bizarre creatures, the journeyman tried nipping his own skin as he walked, in a vain attempt to wake up. His mind had been convoluted in determining what was real or not at times on this trip, thrown up some terrifying pictures and faces that suspended reality but this was surely a nightmare. It had all the hallmarks of one.

Alone in the night, lost and wandering through a cruel world, however, he finally conceded this was probably happening and turned his attention back to his unwitting guide.

Their midnight stroll took them to the top of the hill and further down the other side, through some more trees, before going up again into another clearing.

There, he saw an old mansion. While the cottage at the other end of the forest had been built there straight from a fairy-tale book, this was more like an image from a Victorian novel.

The elfin woman stopped finally and went down onto her knees. In this darkness, it took him a moment or two to register a solitary, white cross planted in the ground. She clasped her hands together and began muttering inaudibly to herself. As he pondered the story to the haunting scene he found himself observing, the elfin woman disappeared into the glowing nothingness she had appeared from.

In the second he glanced away from her she had gone. Only fog remained by the white gravestone. It felt like those moments when you wake up in the middle of the night after only a short while sleeping. When nothing seems real and everything is tinged by a frame of sadness. The faces you picture and the stories behind them, seem like someone else's memories, no matter how well you know them or how much you love them.

Any sad events that come into your mind are not real happenings, to you or anyone else, they are made-up stories. You feel almost as if you are hovering, floating above the world taking a Birdseye view of these memoria, akin to being dead but not departed.

This was exactly how he felt in this moment, that he were dead and merely needed something to confirm it. His thoughts turned to the chaotic nights out that he had grown to loathe. For a while there is nothing as exciting as plunging yourself head on into the clutches of madness, allowing yourself to be thrown to the mercy of the city and whatever lunatics and clowns rule the roost that night.

When all that goes sour it's so hard to get it back and you go seeking something more. It is then you find yourself completely lost and alone, shivering with terror and the icy wind for company, now at the mercy of the wilderness, which is more unforgiving than any cold, wild-hearted city on earth. Should the purpose of this journey be truly to find faith in a romantic spirit existing in the world, this had to mean that somewhere along the road he'd lost elements of love within himself.

As for people just falling out of love, he simply did not believe this, something had to happen to cause it. Everything has a catalyst of some kind. Men and women who leave their partners claiming they simply 'fell out of love' were complete liars and frauds.

Living in close proximity with one person will expose you to all their unremitting faults and their odd habits become great irritants. After a while, every tiny thing that displeases one with the other will feel like a rash that you achingly scratch but never goes away, only spreads and intensifies. The truth being, these people never truly loved each other in the first place and in their desperation and fear, turned a fond affection into love. A neon light into a morning sunrise.

Once upon a time in Barcelona, he got talking to a local who 'fell out of love with football' and did not watch the game for almost four years. He hadn't given up or grown tired at a lack of shiny silver trophies, it was the defection of captain and hero Luis Figo to arch-enemies Real Madrid. From then on, the game would always be tainted by greed, corruption and the sobering thought that the bourgeoisie, the hierarchy will always have the power and therefore will always emerge victorious.

It's easier to blame a perceived mentality of a regime rather than accept you have simply been betrayed. He began to ponder his own Luis Figo moment, nothing sprung to mind and he was forced to accept his own hard truth, that all his morbid self-pity stemmed from the frustration of having never been truly in love.

Reality dragged his mind away from Barcelona – that was for another time, right now he had to think only about survival. Now, he was further away from home than ever, with no guide. How he envied those spiritual people who put their faith in a higher power, be it God or any other celestial being. Woe betide those who looked to political leaders and as for the poor souls who projected their hopes and dreams onto rock 'n' roll stars…

Human beings are fallible and easily corrupted, usually by the lure of sex or money, no matter how good their intentions may once have been.

There was nothing for our fatigued and scared explorer to do but trek, further up the hill and wherever it would take him, if anywhere. As it turned out, he met a river, nothing vast or oceanic, essentially a glorified stream. He kneeled down, cupped some water in his hands and drank. The water was fresh and clear. A group of translucent hermit crabs scuttled past him, as if they were late for something.

Such was the arduous nature of the journey, he had barely noticed the transition from the night to this pleasant, warm sensation by the river. The fog was lifting. The sun looked further away than he had ever seen it, yet he could swear it was glowing red. The gifts of the sky then presented him the thin outline of a rainbow, a symbol of an overwhelming sense of hope.

Whether this good feeling in his heart was the touch of a good spirit, a ray of light as to escaping the seemingly never-ending forest or actually an inner peace that confirmed his own death was as yet unclear. He was too blissful and possessed by joy to care. His thirst quenched, he ignored the aching in his legs and the twists of hunger in his stomach in order to keep going.

There was sure to be a way out, a way back to civilisation. Like being reborn, he at long last, stumbled onto a road and finally collapsed. All he had to do when he woke – if he did – was to wait, eventually someone would drive past and take him to the nearest town, where he could access food, water and clean himself up. Once he had done that, he could attempt to unravel in his mind all the subversive, unnatural horrors he had witnessed and attempt to make sense of this other world he had just passed through.

Sitting on a grass verge by the side of the road, the glorious road back to civilisation, waiting for someone to rescue him, it dawned on him how fortunate he was to effectively breeze through the forest, cold and further confused but unharmed. He could so easily have been murdered by one of the bizarre beings lurking in there. For sure there were more ghouls hiding in the shadows of the trees. Or he could have ended up walking around in circles until he dropped, through hunger or fatigue.

Mercy, mercy was he hungry! And how far had he gone from his vehicle at the lighthouse?

Eventually a pick-up truck stopped by him, though the driver felt the need to interrogate our explorer before letting him in his truck. Everyone is a suspect out here, it was understandable.

Well, he could hardly say he was on a self-appointed journey of romance and had just spent the night running from mermaids and elf ghosts, could he? He told the driver his car had broken down and he had foolishly decided to walk into the forest and had gotten lost.

'That was mighty stupid I guess. Hop in here then.'

When asked how far to the next town and if there was some kind of bed and breakfast, the driver took it upon himself to again be rather difficult.

'Well sure, but don't you wanna go get your car first?'

The traveller explained that he was extremely tired but once he had been fed, cleaned up and rested, he would make enquiries into recovering his vehicle.

'I guess that makes sense. Next town's about twelve miles this a-way, not so picturesque a place, true, but it's got a small hotel I remember.'

With that, he was back on the road. To where, what and why was as open a question as he could possibly ask himself, if what had gone before was a precursor to what was about to be.

The irritating pick-up driver chewed loudly on a fruit bar and made idiotic remarks about the presidency before letting his passenger off in the middle of a street that looked fairly dilapidated.

'Hotel's along that street there I reckon. Be safe now, good luck with your car.'

He thanked his driver and made for the hotel that looked more like a tiny bar with a few rooms above it. Not that he needed luxury of any kind, only rest.

There were two teenagers, a boy and a girl, on the corner of the street. The boy made fairly impressive beatbox noises with his hands and mouth while the girl shouted,

'Change is upon us! We have a future! God Bless Obama!'

He could not help but watch as she performed a rap song dedicated to the new President, a kind of well-wishing to Barack Obama in the style of Lauryn Hill, true street poetry.

"Money is a transitional issue
it matters when you don't have it, it can eclipse you
become your only fear and reason
is it any wonder people turn to thieving
when the dollar is all they have to believe in
The manifesto of get rich then get richer
trample over those beneath you
climb the ladder get there quicker
keep adding those round figures
that's all that matters
your tactics are cloak and dagger
your passion is a dead man
printed on paper, no spiritual saviour
do you not live with the consequences of your behaviour?
or have any belief in yourself?
just measuring everything up to wealth
judge people by their possessions
in the age of Depression, recession, questionable moral professions
will they never learn their lessons?
I may be poor but I'm not paranoid when I say it's all a scam
I believe in sustenance not accumulation
I believe in protection especially for those who have lost direction
in this age where a clique of men can rig an election

for the purposes of money and murder
I read "soldier killed" yet another
The blood is on your hands, the blood is on your hands
fighting terror in far-off lands
when you can't meet the demands
or see that the right to bear arms
has destroyed too many a man
the hopes of a nation have rested on a man with no fear of condemnation
I pray now for the new hope
shy us away from greed
financial gain not our only need
Represent, the present not the descent, into hatred in squalor
A world of acceptance and being decent
things that have been invisible of recent
It is with the deepest sincerity
from the bottom of my heart that I hope you can start to ward off the extremities
educate those who fill their lives with hate
accept your limitations
do not bask in exultations
never back down to intimidations, ignore intimations
do as you do, for they believe in you, pride restored, you've quite a chore
So I wish thee well, and praise the hope anew…"

Her quick, lyrical skills were quite mesmerising, although he conceded that her glare indicated, 'this ain't for you.'

Further down the street, the so-called hotel looked anything but. A licensed brothel, a run-down bar, an activist meeting point, anything but a place to stay. There was no reception and seemingly nobody there. A payphone that looked like it held only an ornamental purpose and a small office space stood before him, but no one was there to greet him. He waited for a moment or two until a woman, somewhere in her mid-fifties, descended from the staircase to the left of what would have been the reception area.

Obviously surprised to have a guest, the lady put on her glasses and started muttering.

'Who are you? No girls today.'

All manner of muttered confusion until the man could eventually enquire about a room. The response suggested to him that very rarely did this establishment receive guests. He could see why, it clearly functioned mainly as a drinking hole for a few sorry souls. It was as run-down as the rest of the town.

Her flapping around made him guess his room was unlikely to be clean and tidy but he cared little, as long as it was hospitable. Gratefully clutching the keys that she had handed him, he laboured up the stairs to his room, believing he would finally be able to rest properly, and at length.

He didn't sleep long. Awoken with hunger and thousands of thoughts inside his head all yearning for reconciliation, he lay there staring at the ceiling and letting those thoughts go down any avenue they felt like going.

Sometimes the mind can go off on such a tangent that it is impossible to retrace your thought process and often you end up with no idea what you were thinking about mere seconds ago. Or at least you think it was seconds, it could be any length of time since you stepped into your mind.

Rummaging around in the drawers next to his bed, he found sixteen cigarettes in a packet and was extremely grateful. He still enjoyed a nice, long, thoughtful smoke every now and then, especially when he had no other company around. Restless of mind, despite the body being a little more relaxed and recharged, a curious conundrum came to his thoughts – so suddenly he had no time to wonder where it came from, he just had to confront it.

How is it possible that a man such as he, finds himself falling out of love with life, displaced from its harmony when he had never really been in love in the first place? 'Love' and 'in love' are of course two totally separate things but this was an interesting idea to ponder over.

He, willing participant or not, was part of a generation that was trying to convince itself that they were all in love. Every crush was an agonising descent into lonely misery that no one else could possibly understand. Every fleeting glance could be an affair, every relationship an all-conquering, triumphant love story and sex had become an evil, lurking yet silent beast. Few seemed to want any association with this beast but through physical necessity, the fear of being alone and the need to feel part of what everyone else is doing meant that everyone was still at it.

Why had he failed to fall in love? As he tried hard to concentrate on a legitimate answer and picture some of the girls he should have fallen in love with, he wondered if perhaps, after all this, he was simply one of those people cursed with the terrible affliction of being unable to truly love.

This, you must understand, is not the same as a person for whom love just never quite happens. (These people, permanently alone, looking downbeat, downtrodden with some weird tick, may seem somewhat pathetic but try imagining this kind of hurt. The pain of never knowing love, having love to give in abundance but no special someone to share it with, ever. They are among the most tragic in all humanity).

Rather, this other kind of person can feel emotional attachments and pleasure, but deep down there is no pure love. Instead, it is replaced by pride or a desire for ownership, usually something self-fulfilling, egotistical.

Then there were the people who loved too much, who were prone to falling in love every day and fabricated a bond or closeness between themselves and others that was never there. The man, so obsessed with love, that he denied himself any chance of ever experiencing it for real.

This got him thinking about the kind of world he truly longed for. A decadent, free society in which everyone was off their heads and dancing to their own beat, their very own rhythm. Expanding their minds and expressing themselves in every possible freeway, no matter how wild or even vulgar it may seem. No boxes, no pigeon-holes, no scenes, no separate societies, no governing bodies, a kind of anarchy without the violence, if such a hope wasn't too paradoxical to grasp.

Or…

A simple, all-natural world in which true love blossomed like the tulips of Holland, where the sky was always blue and the planet thrived on love and charity, sweetness and decency. Genuine kindness instead of abject fear and paranoia.

Could these two utopias co-exist?

Probably not, there was always something waiting to tarnish a paradise. Whichever of these ideal worlds he wished to be part of, his concluding thought on these matters was that love really was the answer, however you wished to look at the statement.

By his watch, the time was only ten fifteen, just over seven hours since he arrived here. He had slept longer than he realised, even if he was not feeling the benefits of it.

So very hungry, he elected to wander downstairs and see about the food and drink on offer. As he reached the bottom of the stairs he could hear the sorrowful plucking of guitar strings and a faint, gruff voice singing along.

"I live my life in night, no place and nobody to call my own
I shoot up bars I'm a Hell's Angel, too bad to be a rolling stone
Too cold to feel the pain of others, I'll sell my soul to get where I'm goin'
I seek no redemption, this hound dog's too far away from home

Hitch a ride to anywhere, my only aim is to flee
No time for the frailties of this life, you can't keep track of me
I haven't the time to talk to you, my life is spent alone
I seek no forgiveness, I'm far too far from home

Should you see me wanderin', don't waste your tears on me
I'm only a dead man walkin', I never really existed you see

The price of life is cheap on the road, livin' by the railway line
I don't care when I die, anytime could be my time
What you see is a ghost, I won't be found at my tombstone
I seek no peace at heart, I'm far too far away from home…"

He joined in the small round of applause as he walked into the bar area where the singers were performing, unsure of how welcome he would be. There was only the patron (whom he had succeeded in startling yet again), two elderly men, one a black man with filthy grey dreadlocks and a beard to match, sitting next to an ill-looking, white man, wearing an even filthier baseball cap. Both gave the impression of rotting. The man with the guitar was a younger fellow dressed in a black suit. The gruff voice he had heard must belong to one of the elderly gentlemen.

'Oh, look it's our guest for the evening,' remarked the landlady, who then offered our traveller a beer and a shot, inviting him to join the party.

'Javier here is from out of town as well. He was putting some songs together for my boys here. He's from Spain,' and she smiled at the Spanish guitar man, possibly the most sexual, suggestive, desiring smile anyone had ever flashed at another person.

She may as well have licked her lips and blew him a kiss.

'Yes it is true. I am from out of town as you say,' said the Spaniard, smiling back at her, although out of politeness rather than attempted seduction.

'I am waiting on a coach that will hopefully arrive shortly after one, to take me further west. I stopped here only for refreshment and ended up singing many songs with these delightful people. They have their own local folk songs which I find quite incredible. I thought such ideas existed only in times long ago.'

He was quite charming, the Spaniard.

'We called him El Mariachi,' piped up the man with the baseball cap, who proceeded to laugh a hideous, toothless hissing laugh, like that of a dog's.

Clearly, he was a man who had devoted his life to alcohol and anywhere he called home, was merely a place to sleep off the effects in between, slowly killing himself in this dive. His buddy had the eyes of a dog rather than the laugh of one, a mad dog waiting for an opportunity to kill. Red with tiredness, sorrow and the drink, they added to his psychotic aura very nicely.

'We sure did. Play us another Javier.' The landlady demanded.

'With pleasure but first I must hear a song, another of the wonderful songs of your town. They are like stories to me,' he replied courteously.

'If it's stories you want, we got one,' spoke the mad dog. 'sing about Victoria, Jim. Sing her sad song.'

His voice was as deep as his eyes were shallow, booming and bass like.

'We haven't sung that in so long, maybe it's too sad for them,' wheezed Jim.

'Our visitors should hear her story. Sing it. I'll join in where I can,' said the woman behind the bar, looking more haggard and old with each rotting minute.

'Okay then. Play away Javier, something sad, quiet.'

Javier strummed gently, merely caressing the strings that brought so much joy to a joyless bar. And they listened to the tragic tale of Victoria Willoughby.

"Victoria was a quiet girl, married Derek at twenty-four
Lived in a house with a bright blue door
A tyre-swing hung in the back yard where yellow flowers grow
A home and a life, all for show

In '83 little Johnny arrived
They swore he would never be deprived
Of love in his life
From a wonderful mother, who was the perfect wife

Another year later another blessing
A bundle of joy, a little girl
They named her Susie and she grew curly hair
An angel they said
Victoria was living in her ideal world
She wasn't to know what lay ahead

Derek began to take to the drink
Got mean and handy with his fists too
The agony she suffered, nobody knew
The bruises would heal
But the pain inside that she would feel
Kept her awake at night

It went on like this for a number of years
Broken bones, the screams and the tears
The perfect life now a world of fear
Johnny got wise when he turned thirteen
Sick of his Daddy being so mean
He got an idea and stuck with the plan

Derek came drunk 'round four in the morning
Just as the day was dawning
Clutching hold of a can of beer
Screamed for Victoria to "get down here!"
He turned on the light to see Johnny there
With a gun in his hand and a mad-lookin' stare

He cocked the gun and pointed it at his dad
Who said "what you gonna do with that?"

Johnny pulled the trigger
His blood ran cold
Victoria howled when she saw the body
She didn't need to be told

Many years later Derek long in the ground
Buried next to his only son
You see little Johnny took his own life
With the very same gun…"

The final line, delivered with no musical accompaniment, sent shivers down his spine. The horrific nature of the story and its graphic detail in song left him in no doubt that these events had actually occurred, but what kind of people sing about them, however mournfully? The mad dog then said something in his slow, booming voice that curdled our man's blood.

'Derek used to sit right there,' pointing to a stool at the end of the bar.

He looked to the Spaniard, who did not seem so disturbed. All he wanted to do was play guitar. Right then, he was sure he had to leave this place, get on Javier's coach or hitchhike, anything to get away. It was nice to be back amongst an altogether human society but this barely qualified as civilisation. This town was where you would come to be murdered. The fumes of death were in the air, the factories closed and stagnant alcoholism replaced their industry. Drinking to remember, then drinking it all away again.

'Perhaps our guest would like to play us a song,' said Javier, diverting the mood of the bar away from its morbidity.

He certainly did not want to play guitar, even though he could, quite competently. Indeed he had even been in a short-lived, folk-type band in his late teens and had even written a couple of songs. His bandmate, a man named Lloyd was one of those chaps for whom music was their entire life and had never quite given up the soundtracks to the hopes and dreams of his youth. Along with music, his other passion was drugs and avoiding work at all costs in order to be under their influence as much as possible.

The duo played mainly open mic nights and even travelled to Amsterdam to play at a fabled music bar there. Lloyd ended up completely out of his eyeballs having acquired drugs in the club and effectively went missing. He had heard a rumour that his obsession with the band 10,000 Maniacs finally overcame him and he himself came to America looking for their original singer Natalie Merchant, but doubted that Lloyd had either the energy or the finance for such a wild excursion. This memory reminded him that he must visit Amsterdam again.

'Well, do you play?' Javier persisted.

As he decided to bite the bullet and play a song for these scoundrels and their new Spanish hero, he elected also to stay one more night and try to rest properly. First thing in the morning he would head off, God knows where, just away from here. Follow the music, for music is nutrition for the soul with hope and this entire escapade was based on a loose thread of hope.

His and Lloyd's back catalogue was hardly extensive but he remembered one in particular, inspired by the man himself and the reprobates and junkies he associated himself with. This song drew its origins from a blackout, when the addicts were deprived of their television set for a matter of hours. So he treated the cultured, the demonic, the decaying and the not-so-tempting temptress to his first live performance in nearly eight years. (You will have to imagine the tune, anything folksy with picking strings will suffice.)

And so the night passed on like this, drinking and singing as if they were old friends. The traveller ended up fairly drunk on gin. Javier departed for his coach around five to one, leaving the landlady distraught and even bitterer than before. She threw out the local drunkards ('til tomorrow) and effectively sent her guest upstairs to his bed.

When he woke the next morning, he felt terrible. Not just the standard, awful hangover feeling in the guts and the forehead, but the sharp terror-tingling all over. He still hadn't eaten. It occurred to him that he had spent most of this journey of romantic discovery in abject fear.

Was he never to escape the ghouls and maniacs that so plagued him? He traipsed downstairs to the sight of no one, probably when the bar looked best. Having already paid for the room the previous night he left immediately through a fire exit, to the next town or city, where love and romance in the modern world would surely be.

Halfway along the street, he saw a homeless man sitting on the ground with a dog and a sign reading 'The War Is Coming', an interesting slant on 'the end is nigh'.

Looking again at the dog, he noticed he was eating something, on closer inspection he could see it was a dead cat. Last night's filth came rocketing through his guts at this sight and he was sick right there on the street, praying that no one had noticed.

Eventually, he found a bus stop and waited there with a heavyset woman who, thankfully, barely acknowledged his probably unwelcome presence and ill manner. Where he was going now, he really had no idea. He would ride the first bus to arrive, until it reached a more civilised part of the world. After fifteen minutes a bus arrived, number 59. He boarded along with his hangover and some truly visceral sights from America flashing before his eyes. These would undoubtedly keep him from sleeping it off on the journey.

How he wished he was on a train, flying through the fields of Belgium and Holland or even next to the cool, calm sea. Neither was the case; urban jungle, after run-down town, decay and deprivation everywhere, in the buildings and the minds of those who populated them.

Tall buildings alerted him that a city must be near. He alighted in the middle of a busy centre and walked through a commercial district, something similar to Glasgow's Merchant City. He craved a cold bottle of beer to settle his shaking nerves and hands. The bar he found did not seem open, maybe it was earlier than he thought. A man polishing the bar seemed slightly aggrieved to have a customer so early but assured him to come in, they were open. The journeyman stared into his green bottle, the bubbles proving quite hypnotic in his weak state.

'Are you here for the concert tonight?' enquired the bartender.

Our man explained that he had made his way here quite accidentally, sparing him any details of events up to this point. He only wanted to hear more about the concert, was this the place he had to follow the music to? Had serendipity led him out of the wilderness into living proof of real love in this world?

'They're from Denmark, so I'm told. Just a one-off show in the back room there to promote a new album, should be a good night. Little disco afterward. Here.'

The bartender handed him a poster advertising the show, a very sixties background of dark pink, sky blue and black stripes that read, 'A one-off performance from THE RAVEONETTES. 9pm.'

The Raveonettes. It swam around in his head; he felt something twitch when he read that name.

'Oh you'll need a ticket. Just fifteen dollars, still got a few behind the bar.'

Excitement rushed through him as he gleefully purchased the ticket. Having never heard of the band until a mere twenty seconds ago, he had no idea what to expect but this did not stop his insides from tingling with anticipation. The barman had never listened to them so could offer no insight into the kind of music that would fill the bar later that night.

'One of our barmaids is a little obsessed with them, she kinda set this whole thing up. She'll be here within the hour if you wanna hold on and have another beer she'll fill you in on them, I'm sure.'

This sounded a reasonable way to kill some time so he ordered another, his hangover waning as the malaise of the previous few days faded from his psyche.

'I'll warn you, she's pretty damn excitable at the best of times so she'll be freakin' unbearable today. She's been bangin' on about tonight for weeks.'

The alcohol mixed with his blood, topping-up the remnants of last night with a gentle, healthy kick. It was still far too early to get blazing drunk again so with the gig in mind, he would have to pace himself and be in good shape for tonight.

Sorrow was finally being replaced with hopefulness. This was the first step of his quest, slowly but surely he would banish all the depressive tendencies and outsider anxieties he held within him. Truth, love and the joy of music would come together and start a revolution in his head. Once he had himself sorted and able to gain personal freedom, he would find the light in the darkness of his mind, open the door to a brave new future of his own…then he would take on the rest of the world.

Starting here, tonight, with The Raveonettes, all the way from Denmark, to save him and everyone else from the wicked taunts and coercions of their demons. Everything that had passed before, would be quite inconsequential, the future was here and now, everyone was a freak and tonight they were going to embrace it and freak out.

The battle for their minds was going to be won by the gentle and decent spirit that brings us all the purest joy in the world, cat prints in the snow, the glow on pregnant women and the sheer splendour of a rainbow. A rescue mission through music.

He knew they were going to be good. What he was experiencing inside of him right there and then was an entirely new emotion – the feeling that the human race was about to be saved and that he was about to fall in love.

At ten to eight, the traveller having whittled away some hours sleeping in a nearby park, the place was rather empty. The excitable girl he had been warned about was an extreme bag of nerves. They had been chatting about the band and tonight's show earlier on, he certainly liked her, although her intensity and nervous energy was quite overpowering, like a plate of food dominated by too much of a spice or dressing.

'Where are they? Where are they?' she kept repeating nervously to herself.

However, it was not the lack of gig-going revellers that was causing her concern, it was the lack of a band, her favourite in the whole wide world. For all she cared, she would stand there by herself and watch them. Shortly, before half past, a crowd had dispersed into the bar and among them waltzed in the striking pair of Sharin Foo and Sune Rose Wagner, known collectively as The Raveonettes, complete with their small entourage, all wearing sunglasses.

'That's them, lo and behold that is them!' she attempted to whisper to the explorer, but this was some form of religious experience for her.

He feared she would need to be sedated before they took to the stage. Off she went, a bouncing ball of raw energy and excitement, to greet her heroes. She emanated a tremendous buzz, sharing his feeling that this show was somehow going to usher in a new generation in time. In truth, he had not expected the main band just to be a boy and a girl and was still clueless as to what kind of music would come out of them, (the girl having neglected to actually let him hear any of their songs, she only spoke – at length – about how fantastic they were and her few descriptions and comparisons gave no clue to their sound).

Dark and beautiful, they fuelled their own enigma.

"Could everyone make their way to the concert area please!" yelled the barkeep.

The anticipation was brimming. The collective energy of the room saw lunatics, freaks and hipsters come together for this moment and when the band finally appeared on to the small, almost makeshift stage, made just for them, to unite all these damaged souls, they would be suspended in time together.

The set began with the woman – the impossibly beautiful half-Danish, half-Chinese, Sharin Foo – working a bassline that married with a thumping drumbeat and drove the song on, the dual vocals echoing and consuming the audience, who instantly become slaves to their music. They were soon grooving to a sleazy, twisting guitar riff that moved them further into the command of the heroes from Copenhagen.

The traveller caught a glimpse of the excitable girl right at the front, blissfully unaware of anybody else as she grooved alone in worship. The third song was like an explosion, everyone knew the words and lost their heads. As he joined the rest of the crowd in jumping around and shouting along to the ballistics harmony coming from the stage, his pre-emptive notions of falling in love tonight came true, he was a fully-fledged devotee to this new kind of love, The Raveonettes and their 'great love sound'.

For the next hour and ten minutes, this little bar's backroom was a temple for this gathering of absurd lives, down-and-outs and fellow hopeless romantics; they were all in love and nothing, absolutely nothing in the outside world mattered. This was real, this was what mattered.

Lost in America, lost as part of the modern world, tonight he found himself. Tonight, he discovered a new reality and it was all thanks to the kind of rock 'n' roll he never thought he would hear, decadent and glorious, screaming pleasure in the dark, projecting the rhythms of their own musical heroes, every song becoming symbolic of a soundtrack to a new future. The time of the raving, mental love generation was here, it had arrived.

For the first time in his entire life, he felt privileged to be a part of the world. Sometimes, it can be a very wonderful place.

If this soulful contingent could take this mentality out of the bar into the world outside, they could all be free. Free to love, free to let loose, free to see through all the hypocrisy and bullshit (including their own), rise up against the politics of war and smash down the walls their captors had built for them. Unwitting prisoners bursting free and claiming a future they knew they deserved. Inspired by the rock 'n' roll of the past being reborn, all the while singing as they raved.

The great tragedy was that such a mindset was unlikely to be able to exist out with this room. Eventually the band would stop playing and leave the stage, the people going back to their lives of anger and disillusionment, accepting their fates as if this had never happened.

They ended with a wild, hands-to-the-sky disco-rock anthem that seemed to cry: "Go out and live free!"

The message would fall on deaf ears. He knew it. The glory of this night would be just another memory come morning. The party continued in the room, the band even joining their adoring crowd, Gods among mere mortals.

The traveller spoke with the girl, who was floating on air. Vacant as if she had truly been transported to another planet. By now, everyone was out of their minds on drugs and alcohol and disco music. They all looked immensely beautiful under the flashing lights and vague neon dim. He would join them on the dance floor, share this night and prolong these moments as long as he possibly could. It wasn't at all what he had envisaged but he had found love and romance after all, in a crowded little room where people were dancing and loving each other because they wanted to, because they all felt the same thing and not because they felt obliged to pretend like they were having fun. These people weren't just having fun, they were having a collective mental breakdown in the most positive of ways. Dancing like a freak along with everyone else, he caught a glimpse of the girl leaning against the wall, arms folded across her body, surveying the scene she had helped create.

She appeared to brush a tear from her eye as she turned and walked out the door. He watched her for a moment or two, still dancing, until a strange man in a white suit accosted him on the dance floor. This man had an otherworldly air about him, as if he were not really there, an illusion on the dancefloor. The illusion spoke to him.

A hallucination of his conscience perhaps, another altogether terrifying apparition. As with all things, they must end. The disco was beginning to go to sleep and telling everyone else to do the same. They were alone again, fearful and lost. Strangely, he thought of the girl he had seen that night in Glasgow, forever anonymous to him. She would have enjoyed this. Some people pass us by, our lives intertwine for mere moments but their faces stay in our minds. The would-be love affairs and friendships denied a chance to bloom thanks to the inhibitions and suspicions, things that needn't exist and certainly were not evident tonight.

Outside, the world was crumbling around itself.

A revolt had begun. This was no pleasure rampage of football hooligans or displeased student protests, this was a full-scale riot intent on bringing down society. Every window was smashed, every car damaged. Fires were breaking out all over the place and it looked like some especially fierce maniacs were deploying explosives. Many had guns. It appeared to have been going on for many hours but could only have erupted in the last two or less, escalating phenomenally quickly.

This was planned, not quite on this scale, perhaps not, but somebody had definitely planned to create a major disturbance here tonight. Somebody had no hope for the change ahead and wanted to create their own vision for the world, one of devastation and control.

For all the rage, there seemed to be fairly few acts of looting and violence towards civilians. There didn't seem to be any civilians, only anarchists. It was the buildings of commerce and enterprise that were the target here, the complete obliteration of it all, their relentless intent. Even if the police were able to get to them now, they would need an incredible amount of numbers and force. There must have been at least four hundred out there, a testament to the organisational skills or inspiring terror of their leader. Either way a master of sedition, whoever they were. Months, possibly even years of scheming and networking must have been dedicated to this.

Whether all these people had conspired to come here together and bring it all down or whether a few militant madmen had swept everyone else up in a tidal wave of mass destruction was unclear as yet. While just a few minutes before he had been part of a crowd losing its mind to music he now found himself contained within a mob of vigilantes losing their minds in the most primitive form. This was revolution at its most basic level – create as much damage and violence as possible until you are stopped, if you can be stopped.

A thought struck him, what if this roving lunatic asylum had taken over elsewhere? Surely if one possesses the skills and the knowhow to orchestrate a planned riot, he or she would not limit themselves to one tiny corner of society.

People WERE angry, people were sick and tired of those in charge, fed-up of being trodden on and told that they were nothing, little more than subservient drones, just ones and zeros in the machine of the government. Living, breathing tools designed only to add noughts to their bank balances. It could feasibly take just one man to tell them that they were worth more than that.

They need not submit to all they have been told to get down on their hands and knees for, that they were not servants, they too can be seen, heard, even feared. With the correct oratory skills and leadership qualities, a capacity for hate and violence, you could get the drones of the banks and building societies to become your own drones, simply call them soldiers. Hell, call them heroes if it will get them to do what you want.

But he couldn't rationalise any further, he had to get out of here. Again, trapped. By fear or by the elements, mystic madness or the company of maniacs, he always found himself trapped by something, with no option but to run. In some ways, he admired these rioters, instead of seeking some personal fulfilment or any other form of escapism they had fought their captivity and their captors head on, with brute force.

In this case the probable target for the rebels being the long sought-after powers that be. And they were being fought with a maniacal, swivelling index finger and explosives. He could not join them though, because he knew how this would inevitably end – in what their leader, for they must have one, would deem a 'blaze of glory', nothing more than a fanciful and misguided term for being shot dead. Once enough were killed (and they would be, eventually) this nightmare that was someone's dream would be over.

At this moment, he was taking refuge behind an overturned car as debris and glass came crashing down around him. He could see two men on the top floor of a building, launching filing cabinets, computers and all manner of office supplies from the window, crying: "Look out below!"

To his left he saw one man blow up a post-box and in the corner of his eye caught two other men jump from a moving car that went on to plough its way through the display window of a shop. What kind of shop, he could not identify, everything was burning or somehow destroyed. From the ensuing explosion he guessed an electrical store.

Some of these men must have believed they were fighting for a cause, however skewed a view they had of going about it. Others clearly just wanted to destroy and take pleasure in seeing everything coming to an end. Were the authorities not even going to try and stop them?

The girl from the concert! She was there, he saw her! He crawled over and grabbed her, pulling her to the ground to hide with him. Maybe she knew what was going on, maybe she had some answers. Something and someone had caused this mayhem and everything, he knew, had a catalyst. He wanted to know the trail to the catalyst and somehow, he figured that she knew something. He screamed above the riot and asked what was going on here.

'There's no use talking here! Are you okay?' He could barely hear her.

Just then, a man on top of a car started shouting through a megaphone, gaining the attention of most of the mob. Any hopes that this were some kind of police negotiator were dashed as he listened to the echoing words of the demented drill sergeant. Not all of his hateful, violent words rang clear but as he turned to the girl, now holding her head in her hands – through shame or fear – he realised for certain that she was involved in all this in some way.

Had the life affirming concert simply been a diversion? She knew who that lunatic spewing madness from his megaphone was and perhaps had assisted him, unaware of the full extremities he was willing to go. His words were vitriolic poison and contained no hints that this was going to stop until somebody did something major to stop it. There was no spirit in a rainbow to save these souls. They wanted the fear to spread, to breed, they wanted the power. And they believed they were going to achieve it.

'They're going to try and take the rest of the city now, we need to get to the safe place. There's a minibus waiting in the car park at the back of the bar, on my say, so run to the bar but stay low.'

He asked her about the people who lived here, other civilians left behind to perish in the mayhem. It was one thing destroying buildings representative of a hated system but what about people's homes and lives?

'There's no time! Most people are safe now go!'

Across the warzone and through the bar they went, somehow managing to avoid the fire that looked set to engulf the whole place.

'RUN!'

At the other side, the bus was still there. They climbed inside and sped off. Small explosions were going off in the bar. The traveller prayed that the crowd of loving revellers had all escaped safely. Only moments ago they were celebrating the birth of a new love generation. Even if they didn't fully realise it, they certainly felt it, now many of them may just have been blown up. He prayed not and wondered about this 'safe' place and why he was trusting this girl at all.

'It's a small area near the shore, shrouded by trees. Like a big canal. They're using it as some kind of holding pen 'til they know what to do with them. Most of the citizens were evacuated there before they went crazy. They won't kill them.'

He wasn't so sure, she sounded as if she were trying to convince herself of this.

'There will be guards there making sure no one escapes or police get in, but we'll be safe.'

He looked at her, intensely focused on driving, avoiding his stare. His look was part of disbelief and some revulsion, how could he not be suspicious?

'Look man, just trust me, I will explain this as best I can but right now you just have to trust that I'm trying to protect you.'

Suitably far away from the images of violence and explosions, the memory of the madness now seemed as surreal as the metamorphic murder bar or the grieving elfin woman, silently weeping in the fog.

They drove across a long bridge and she began to describe the origins of the riot. As he suspected, the man with the megaphone had been her lover.

'It all started after Bush was elected the first time. We were still in college and had all the great student ideals of the world. He was a real patriot and couldn't believe that his country could let him down by rigging an election, the presidency of all things. He set up this movement, as most people in college here do and I joined up. It wasn't much at first, maybe ten of us, small protests, newsletters, that kind of thing. I didn't think much of it and we kind of lost interest once we started being boyfriend and girlfriend. That was more important and we realised that a few college kids weren't going to fix the presidency. Then there was Afghanistan and Iraq, which got him all worked up and in the revolutionary spirit again. More protests, marches. When Bush got re-elected he went fuckin' nuts. He and his buddy, his sort of second-in-command were on top of a building threatening to jump unless there was a recount. Some others got involved before they all got arrested. He's got that dangerous mix of being utterly charming and horribly persuasive. I didn't want to see him end up in jail so I asked him to let it go, one man cannot force change in the way he was hoping to. That was it for a little while, I would see him reading 'The Art of War' and other military books similar to that, one about James Connolly, some I.R.A. guy. I didn't want to read too much into it, it was obviously something he was interested in so I kept quiet. Then his friend's cousin got blown up in Afghanistan and that was it. Pamphlets again, everything on a bigger scale. His friend's cousin was just an excuse though, he was looking for a catalyst. Soon he was holding secret meetings, convincing himself he was in a war. He became so secretive, so distant so I broke it off for a while. I tried to confront him about what he was doing but of course he wouldn't tell me anything. We didn't really stay in touch until I told him about the Raveonettes coming here to play and he admitted he was planning something. Something good, taking the protests up a notch. I was worried sure, but he told me not to be, that he had faith in Obama like everybody else and just wanted to send a message saying that the people were the ones who held the real power. The more hints he dropped and secret conversations I overheard I suspected more and more but I didn't imagine that, if I did I just didn't want to admit to myself. I honestly don't know if that's what he wanted. He's lost his mind.' A tear glistened from a sad, regretful eye, glistening intensely until it fell and disappeared back into her skin. 'He won't stop until he is stopped. He's probably going to die…and those people…it's my fault. I could have stopped it.'

Only it wasn't her fault. True, perhaps she could have prevented the madman unleashing his demons but it must be difficult to stand in the way of someone that you love, especially if they are swept up in revolutionary sentiment. Maybe it seemed a bit romantic, that thrill of danger and feeling like you're part of something. He certainly knew how amazing that felt.

Somewhere along the line he had lost his will to peaceful protest and unseen political manoeuvrings and true to the form of his own government, decided to attack. The powers that be will never listen to words or idle threats, they only pay attention to action, violent action. Emmeline Pankhurst knew it, Al-Qaeda know it today. Again, he and the megaphone maniac probably weren't so different, both yearning for a better world, a change in attitudes, clinging to hope that had nowhere to grow. You could go seeking a better world or you could do something about the one you are in.

'Do something,' of course being the vaguest of terms. Something could be marches, newsletters, protest groups or it could be organising a mass riot sweeping across the state. Love had failed to ease his troubled mind; words couldn't quell the fire in him so he struck back. Sitting here with his former lover, he hoped the madman would be remembered for this. Although he was encouraging, participating in, even leading terrorism (against his own country no less) and undoubtedly so disillusioned and misguided so as to become completely insane, he hoped it would be not be in vain, that these efforts would count for something at least, his message to those in charge that the source of true power comes from the people themselves would be heard. He hoped America would remember this night, just as he would, only for completely different reasons.

4

'We're nearly there,' she said, as they parked the bus at the back of a warehouse, more than likely not in use. 'We just have to go through this underpass and it will take us to the Shore where they're keeping people. Like I said there will be guards, about fifty I think, so just let me talk to them.'

The Shore, this safe place, held no redemption for him. He was caught up in the worst nightmare yet, one so painfully real with such a bleak outlook, nothing fantastical about it that could convince his tired mind he was actually dreaming. It occurred to him he might never get home now. The guards would hold him here forever, a hidden, sealed off watery alcove in the middle of an industrial wasteland. Of course they might just kill him instead.

'Do you hate me?' she asked him bluntly.

While he could not say that he knew her so well and even so, hate her and what she had helped to cause would be fairly justified at this time. But he didn't hate her, he couldn't. This current situation of militant rule and the fact she was now leading him to what essentially sounded like an open-air holding pen, was so fearful and bizarre that he hadn't found time to think properly and make sense of it all, least of all emotional decisions.

This blonde, twitchy girl, whom he had only met the previous day, had already inadvertently saved his soul and was now making efforts to save his life. Whatever her involvement in the fact that it needed to be saved in the first place seemed somehow irrelevant. Those were the facts. They came out of the underpass to be pleasantly greeted by a man pointing a rifle at them.

'Who's there? Explain yourself! I'll fuckin' shoot!'

Luckily, her knowledge of the safe place and her claim that the traveller was "on our side" was enough to prevent them being shot and allowed into the refuge, where they joined scores of others. The scale of this operation got more astonishing. The scene of the last town may have looked like a thoughtless rampage yet the planning that must have gone into the strategy of all this was staggering.

Admirable too that the relative safety of citizens had been considered and a refuge set-up rather than simply killing them. Unless this was another part of the coup de control, a device to show what they were truly capable of. Not that any of this was in any way enjoyable, except the girl's company, if this could be called such.

They sat on a small hill looking at the brown, peaceful water, an occasional ripple bubbling through it. People around them huddled together, they were crying, taking shelter and comfort from one another. It was all they had left. Many would have witnessed the destruction, their small part of this vast land obliterated without warning or reason. They were the unfortunate and innocent first targets of a madman's disgraceful plan, others were possibly suffering the same fate right now. More refugees would be arriving soon, more confused and bewildered prisoners, waiting here for who knows what. The traveller who, suffice to say was finally regretting this journey, ached for a solution and to sleep, a resolve of any kind.

'I need to find out what's going on. Wait here, I'll come back for you I promise.'

As she walked away to try and get some answers to this horrible scenario, he realised that he hadn't even caught her name. Between excitement and terror, salvation and explosions, too much had being going on for a simple, polite exchange of names. Maybe he would learn it in a newspaper when this was all over, if she failed to keep her promise.

He was alone again, every memory he ever had, every face in his mind, floated away on the water without a reflection. Hopelessness reigned again, anger and loss consumed, he felt like he would rather be part of the rioting than stuck here, watching all his aspirations die.

The end was almost definitely in sight now. May as well try and sleep until the girl came rushing back, more excited than ever to tell him the nightmare was over.

In his dreams, he saw every picture return from the water for him to see one last time, a succession of happy endings to sweeten the images. He saw Spanish Lara dancing the flamenco, his friend Lloyd shacked up with Natalie Merchant, his mother growing herbs from a windowsill, the murderous demons and priests, the lonely lighthouse keeper and anonymous Mary in a nightclub, still dancing.

This time he spoke to her, he loved her. He saw snow putting out a fire on a lake and prayed this was a metaphor for the solution to the nightmare out with his subconscious. Sweet voices were singing to him from faraway lands. Fully aware he was only dreaming, he didn't want to wake up, to be back there, lost and lonely on the shore of no hope.

The rain came and woke him. Nobody cared about the downpour of water droplets from above, it was hardly going to make a difference to their situation. He thought about his grandparents back in Poland and the atrocities they suffered, on a much wider and unimaginably more horrific scale than this. At least these people hadn't been slaughtered, yet. His grandfather had never spoken to him about what happened and he never considered it his place to ask. That was something that of course would always stay with you and must never be forgotten but if someone who was actually there wishes to block it from the forefront of their mind and bury it deep down inside, as best they can, then that is absolutely their right.

He wished not to think about this any further and wondered again about the girl. The more time went by, the unlikelier it was she was coming back.

A man nearby to him was staring into the distance, vacant and hollow, paying no attention to the downpour. Perhaps he was thinking similar thoughts as the traveller, probably they all were. He must have felt eyes on him as he turned his head in the direction of the traveller, their eyes catching each other's, two lonely men who had lost everything, waiting in real-life purgatory by the waterfront.

This man had Latin American qualities about him as he advanced toward our explorer, sporting a bald head and impressive handlebar moustache, his open shirt displaying a tattoo of another man's face on his chest. His slow, hunched walk made him seem as threatening as the foreboding reek of hopelessness that had replaced the rain in the air.

'Were you looking at my tattoo bro?' enquired the Latin American. True, he had noticed it as he came toward him (it was hard not to after all) but he had not been able to see it when he first noticed him, so he said no, truthfully.

'This is not just any man you know. This is not a former lover, if that's what you are thinking. I am not like that.'

The traveller began to wonder if he had said something to the man to cause him to be so defensive and hostile but remembered saying only 'no'. Out here, even in this warped situation, things could still get stranger.

'This…is my brother,' he said dramatically, hitting his chest after the word, brother. 'My brother was a great man, is still a great man. Do you have a brother my friend?'

Not so certain he was definitely a friend of this man he again replied only monosyllabically, but a truthful one at least – no, again. He did have an older sister but didn't feel he needed to share this information. Was he finally meeting his maker? This man looked like a killer.

'Then you cannot know how I feel about my brother. As I told you, he is a great man. An adventurer, a socialist, a fighter. A man who believed in things that made people think him mad. Genius, not mad.'

He lit a cigarette with a match and how our explorer yearned for one.

'I must ask you sir, what do you believe in?'

He told him he wasn't sure anymore. He thought that he believed in love and music but the situation he now found himself in made him think that the overwhelming power that would rule us all was the hatred and violence of man.

'Very good. I believe that too. Would you like a cigarette?' the Latin extended his arm to hold out a tin of smokes, the traveller gratefully taking one and his latest companion lit it for him. 'The world is a dark place. We symbolise all humanity, you and I, alone in the outdoors, the rain settling on our skin, only our beliefs to guide us through. I must ask you another question, do you believe in guiding spirits?'

He thought back to his moment in the airport and to the rainbow that guided him out of the forest. Once again he spoke truth,

'Yes I do.'

'Good, in this sense we are kindred spirits ourselves. Please, let me tell you about my brother.'

The traveller acquiesced, still in gratitude for the cigarette and now very interested in the man who wore his heart on the exterior of his chest.

The traveller had no idea with what to make of the South American's (to be precise, Argentinian's as he had now discovered) tale, so he stayed silent on the matter. Especially when he saw a tear rolling down the face of the Argentine.

'Forgive me sir, I can get quite emotional when I speak of my brother. I feel very tired now so I must sleep until we are released. They cannot keep us here forever can they? No I'm sure not. I hope to see you again before we leave. Thank you for your time sir.' And with that, he went back to where he had been before and fell asleep sitting up.

The rain had long ceased but there was no sun as daylight approached. Where was the girl? The harshest of realisations that he hadn't yet been willing to admit to himself had come true, she wasn't coming back, not now. Whatever happened to her, whether she escaped or was let go or God forbid, was killed (no gunshot had been heard so took some comfort in that this was unlikely) she wouldn't be coming back for him. She wouldn't keep her promise.

The loneliness was crushing, the hopeless fear palpable. He did not share the Argentine's optimism that they would be allowed to leave this place. Why go to the trouble of bringing them all here just to release them back into society, albeit a (perhaps) changed society? For most of these poor souls there was no place to go back to, their homes had been destroyed, the stores and buildings in which they worked burnt down. He was desperate to know what was going on out there but nobody had any idea and the guards (if they even knew themselves) certainly weren't going to tell anyone, not the true situation anyway. The sun was making a small effort to come through the stolid early morning clouds and as our explorer caught a faint glimpse of a beam, it triggered a pounding sadness in him.

Almost without realising he was weeping softly, his head between his knees, praying to go home. There were others praying, he even saw some people gathered round an out-of-place, wishing-well dropping pennies into it, such was the desperation for any form of hope. The Argentine still slept, although by now he was lying down.

Suddenly…an explosion was heard. And another! Everyone was alert; guards stationed on a small bridge at the other side of the refuge were running towards the commotion, panic and confusion gripped them all. Now came the time for these lost souls to revolt against THEIR captors! As the guards rushed to tackle the explosion and investigate its origins, it became clear a couple had been killed in it. Their numbers had dwindled, they still had their guns but a few brave souls could wrest them from the remaining ones, there could only be eight or nine now.

Maybe the people could have challenged them before the explosion but in the climate of fear they had created, it needed a catalyst to excite them into a fight for survival. One of the brave souls was the Argentine, who had leapt up from his slumber, seized a gun and shot the guard who had owned it, perhaps he was versed in war (that would explain his sleeping sitting upright).

He was screaming like a general, ordering people to,

'Move! Get out!'

There was only one way out, over the bridge to the disused industrial site on the other side. Three women were forcing one guard into the wishing well, his screams echoing as he crashed to the bottom, two men launched another into the murky water. The Argentine had shot another guard and was making his way to the bridge. His eyes had noticed a huge water container in the wasteland with a linked stairway from the fire escape that provided a route to the top of the building.

'Climb the fucking steps! Get on the fucking roof! Get attention! Move! Fucking move!'

People were probably terrified of him but he was trying to save them. It was quite a sight to behold. In mere seconds, hundreds of people who had abandoned hope revolting in a frenzied bid for survival, urged on by yet another madman, of the good sort this time. All it needed was a classical score, a symphony to silence his screaming.

Once everyone was safely across the bridge he went looking for the remaining guards, toward the scene of the explosions. The traveller was helping people up the fire escape as the Argentine had instructed, although most would have to stay on the ground for fear of the ladders breaking or the entire container collapsing.

Amazingly, it seemed as if no civilians had been killed. Eventually, the Argentine joined him on the roof, a little scraped but generally okay.

'The girl I saw you talking with sir, she was your wife? Lady friend?' He again replied no to him, saying he didn't even know her name.

'Well it does not matter. I am afraid to report that it seems she was the one who caused the first explosion and was either shot or died setting it off. Her face was badly burned but I recognise it was her. She is a martyr.' He yelled to everyone on the roof and down below. 'She is our hero! She saved us! She is a true heroine!'

He thumped his chest, the face of his brother.

'What now?' someone asked.

'Now? Now we will wait, try to get attention. It will not be long. Until then we will thank God for this woman.' The girl had kept her promise after all.

The Argentine fired a shot into the air and descended the stairs to re-join with the survivors on the ground, all the while shouting: 'She is our hero!'

The traveller looked out at the world in front of and below him, grieving for the loss of her and lamenting the events of the past few hours and of all the past, all things were lamented by all who were there in this moment. The lives that could have been, the death of love in today's society, the general state of the world. From up here, the whole image looked like it was made out of silhouettes.

Finally, the wait was over. It felt like it had been growing into years they were up there. The police and ambulances arrived, taking the survivors as they were to be called to proper refuge, some were taken to hospitals, the fallen guards to the morgue.

The Argentine fled, he was a hero but doubted the police would take that view. Some people asked to go home, forgetting that their homes – if they still stood – were in the middle of a crime scene. The traveller asked about the girl and if they had stopped the riots but no one was giving any answers yet, he probably would have to read about it after all.

A police officer asked him where he was going; he had absolutely no idea. Home, wherever that was for him now. He was taken to the hospital as they believed he was suffering from shock trauma. He didn't wait around for the doctors to say they had found nothing wrong with him and discharged himself. Out in the streets again, he went to find a newspaper stand to see if there were any initial reports of the mayhem and its aftermath.

One local paper ran a headline 'RIOT CAUSES HUNDREDS TO FLEE' which contained very little information. Nothing he wasn't aware of already. It did say the police had arrested a number of men connected with the disturbances (a much understated term for what he had witnessed) and safely assumed they must have been stopped. No news about the girl, no name, no photograph. She was dead, that was all really needed to know, and her name didn't really matter. He threw the paper away.

Sitting on the steps outside an apartment block he plotted his next move. Oddly enough he didn't feel the urge to get home anymore, possibly because he wasn't sure where he was going to return to yet. He felt like a survivor. As a survivor he owed it to himself to make one last journey and in his head there was only one possible destination for a man who felt like owed himself something – Amsterdam.

The next flight wasn't for four hours so after purchasing his ticket and some cigarettes, he had plenty of time to ponder what he would do there (other than get high), how long he would stay (not long) and most of all pray that it wouldn't turn into a procession of surreal nightmares like this adventure stateside had. He chain-smoked outside the airport as he reflected on these events and what kind of future was in store for a ruined world.

Before he knew it, he was here in Amsterdam. This time he wasn't looking for love or a new hope, just somewhere to relax and bask in his new found sense and appreciation of freedom. The love he had so sought wasn't found in any individual tales of romance, only in a collective spirit. Love was more of an energy than a feeling. You had to look for it and even then you might only find it with a little slice of serendipity, or by complete accident. You may find it in a ghostly wilderness, in the lusting of forgotten souls, inked on the chest of a strange hero. It could be in the music two Danish rockers played on a night that would be remembered for all the wrong reasons, for destruction rather than creation.

It was in the salvation of a girl who was willing to sacrifice the lives of hundreds for the sake of her own, selfish love – only to then save those people. Love probably couldn't conquer all, not even siege mentality could do that. One certainty about love was that it could destroy everything if people convinced themselves they felt it strongly enough. At the same time, it probably could save you.

Taking a stroll through the magnificent Vondellpark, he managed to salvage some hope for the world. One man could not and would not change everything, a collective mentality was needed, a belief in an altogether similar ideal. They had went about it in completely the wrong manner and ultimately, thankfully, failed but those rioters had the right basic idea, if not the mentality.

Show the world (in their case the nation at least) that people in numbers could achieve what they were looking for. However, simply smashing things up with no real plan or agenda is unlikely to achieve anything. To succeed, you must be united with a clear aim. Anger and discontent were a good fuel but not a cure. Get your message across but don't simply destroy things.

Mindless violence would get you nowhere, one must have patience and opportunism, particularly if your aims are revolutionary in spirit. Human nature doesn't have much time for patience. We generally want it all and want it all now.

As strange as it may seem, The Raveonettes were to be the abiding memory of the trip rather than the various near death experiences he had endured, possibly because even now the Danes were the only thing that seemed truly real. The brushes with doom and disaster were a positive now, it showed him that something or someone was watching over him and hopefully would continue to do so. With the Raveonettes, he instantly fell in love. Something that powerful will stay you forever, long after bars close and riots die down.

He knew for sure love was real, however his actual experience of it differed from his hopes and expectations. He would see them again someday, somewhere, just as he knew the heroic Argentine would see his beloved brother again when he returned from invading Hell, whatever that actually meant.

The paths we take to our discoveries, however insignificant on the grand scale of things are usually taken blindly and often lead us back to exactly where we were but it is the experiences that count.

If he were to die tomorrow he would be incredibly grateful for every experience on his journey, not just in America but in his whole life. Right now, the only path he was taking was the route home.

As he strolled, he saw a rasta man with the same sickly, hollow eyes as the man who sang songs about sons killing their fathers in a bar he went into and died every night, he spotted a bald man with a moustache and a touch of Latin American about him, lonely men and excitable girls. His world was about people, not places. There are no real refuges or naturally romantic lands, but there are real heroes, real Gods among us, real spirits guiding us home and that was where he was going.

He reached Dam Square and waited only two minutes for the number five tram. Finally, he was on his way home. There was a conflict of many emotions; melancholy, a sense of loss, overwhelming tiredness but overall he was delighted to be going home.

A displaced person, such as he, will always struggle to feel at home in most places but his experiences had taught him that home is ultimately where you belong and that was not the strangest backroads in all of America nor was it the wild streets of Glasgow.

Who knew where home was, where he belonged, but not chasing the impossible dreams he had once believed in. He would leave that all behind, he knew the truth he needed to know about love and romance in the modern world and that would be enough for him. He had seen and witnessed things that pushed reality to the absolute limit. It was now in the real world and this was where he was finally going, after this incredible journey, this trip into the absolute and fearful unknown. And he had survived.

5

As he landed, it took him a little while to figure out exactly how long he had been away. Most definitely it was not as long as it felt. It seemed like an age, the events of the trip making it seem like he had been to altogether different worlds. At so many points he wondered if he was ever going to get out and be able to go home. He worked out that he had only been away for eleven days.

People would ask him about his trip and he knew the only thing, the only truthful thing at least, he would tell them about the band he had seen on the night of the riots. He wondered if news of that had reached over here, even if it had, it was unlikely to be a big story. Disturbances and heroes occur every day on some scale, do they not? He longed to hear Billie's voice, he wouldn't feel properly at home until he did.

Already the United States seemed a distant memory, so much had been detached from reality. How he wished he had a photograph of the girl who saved his life. For all she may well have helped instigate the destruction, she gave him the greatest feeling, the best night and the most insanely brilliant music of his life. For this, and her eventual heroics he would love her always.

She could have left him there on that shore and saved herself from the violence and the consequences she would undoubtedly have to face, but she didn't, she came back for him and protected him as she promised.

The romantic in him wished to believe that she died for him, as these must be the most romantic words anyone could ever say but he knew this wasn't true. She didn't die for those other people on the shore either, she died to redeem herself. Love took her to the brink of being an accessory to many murders and ruined lives but the overwhelming spirit of it brought her to martyrdom.

For whatever reasons, the pair were designed to meet on that unforgettable night and save each other, without even learning the other's name. That was his love story, his own, just as the events he became a part of, across the water were memories in his own private universe. She was dead and gone but she would live within him and through the king and queen of their own little universe, the Godlike geniuses from Denmark.

Their music would forever remind him of the power of free, united peoples. He felt sorry for anyone who wasn't there that night, when love and anarchy met under a blanket of amazing music. His path had been and would continue to be a long and trudging one but at least it would always have that music. He stepped out into what finally felt like a semblance of the real world.

Under the bright lights and a velvet skyline, the hustle-bustle commotion of the airport and the frantic noise of the streets out there, his mind was finally at ease. Thinking of the nameless faces he had encountered and the ghoulish, hateful fragments of human nature, of which love had sadly become one.

He had foreseen humanity's demise in many forms and knew it was only a matter of time and chance before one of them came true. All he had seen were merely visions in a crystal ball, distorted by the limitations of the human brain to suspend belief.

His heart panged for the girl and the Argentine, for the knowledge he would probably never again feel the way he did in that briefest of moments in history. And for Mother Nature, who had rescued him and was forced to watch as humanity relentlessly fucked and killed its way to its own oblivion. Its flaws and fallibilities were the same the whole world over but he was determined to be different.

He was no hero, nor he was exceptional or unique, just a person who had seen and felt things most never would. The spectrums of fear and love had a different meaning to him. Those nine days in America would very soon appear like someone else's life and he knew in years to come he would still struggle to believe most of it ever happened, the music and love that he had eventually found there would be proof, if not living. He disappeared with his unique memories into the city lights, to spread the word and maybe, just maybe, make a small change to this world that finally, he was delighted to be part of.